THE ARRANGEMENT 25
THE FERRO FAMILY

H.M. WARD

H.M. WARD PRESS

The Series with Over 13 MILLION Copies Sold

H.M. WARD

NEW YORK TIMES BESTSELLING SERIES

THE ARRANGEMENT 25

The FERRO Family

Copyright © 2019 by H.M. Ward

LAREE BAILEY PRESS

First Edition: Feb 2019

ISBN ebook: 978-1-63035-232-5

ISBN paperback: 978-1-63035-233-2

THE ARRANGEMENT 25

CHAPTER 1

MANHATTAN, NEW YORK

STANDING on the penthouse balcony later that night, I rest my palms on the thick metal railing to let the coldness bite into my skin. Swallowing hard, I peer down at the cars below with their red lights blinking as they crawl forward an inch and stop. The sounds of the city were once a symphony of delight. I loved it here. Now it's noise. Heavy and oppressive. Sighing deeply, I lift my eyes to the park across the street, allowing my gaze to skim the treetops looking for something to settle on—something to make me feel grounded. Anything that allows me to know I'm anchored. Safe.

The treetops look like jagged fingers of an ancient witch. They wiggle, casting spells and coldness. There's nothing. Nothing solid to see and tether me to sanity. I feel the frayed edges of my mind weeping. They cry out day and night, "Remember what you've done." It's become an ominous chant that never ceases. The blood on my hands will never dry, never wash away. There's a reason why I haven't mentally shattered all over Manhattan. A reason why I must find a way to continue. I place my palm on my expanding belly.

I will not break. For them. For Sean. For me. I will not break. The words are a whisper in my mind worn thin from overuse. Still, it's all I have holding me together.

Closing my eyes, my mind wanders, retreats to the place where calmness floods my veins. Inhaling the crisp air deeply, I release my stranglehold on the railing and finally, I can see it in my mind's eye—feel it. It's like I'm back at that beach house, padding down a path lined with smooth stepping stones. Indigenous flowers line the edges of the stone walk, jutting up from the sandy earth in plumes of blue and pink. The sounds of waves lapping the shore fill my ears, but I still can't see the ocean.

My mental stroll continues as I pass the clear blue pool that lies directly outside the floor to ceiling windows of the great house. The waters glow turquoise as sunlight kisses the ripples of the pool, scattering sparkles.

A memory slashes through my daydream, and forces its way in. Ribbons of blood fill the gem-colored water before the bodies appear, floating face down. That night, I thought I lost Sean. I thought that was him.

It wasn't Sean. He's alive. We are both alive and home. Tightening my eyes, I shake the memory away.

Meditation is important. It's become part of my life. Dr. Chan told me to focus, not to let the numbness overtake me again. She doesn't realize I'm at an impasse. I can accept my past if I allow the lack of feeling to overtake me, but if not—I can't.

Accepting what I've done will destroy me. As it is, my mental state feels fragile, weak. I hate being this vulnerable.

The irony of the moment is so bitter, I want to spit. Shaking my head, I back up and sit on a fluffy blue chair with ornate scrolling on the arms. Then I lean back against a tufted leather pillow that's buttery soft. Lowering my head, I cup my face with my hands and swallow the sobs that want to cry out. This is who I wanted to be when I met Sean. I wanted this. The eternal numbness. To feel nothing. To be ruthless. I would have traded my soul to get it. Maybe I did, because my insides feel so hollow right now.

Fight, Avery. Push it back. My inner voice chides, weak, but not entirely gone. The blissful numbness that I desired most is here but I no longer want it. The problem is, part of me craves that sense of nothingness. The void that would swallow me, assuage my guilt, and leave me to move forward with my life. It's the easy path. One step down that road and I won't come back, but it beckons to me. Calling out like a lifeline that can save me when all others have failed.

I will not break.

Sean is no longer barren of emotion. There are moments that come like a reflex where he chokes it out, but then something within him changes. He can release the feeling and share it with me. Show other people. Even the assholes on the street who think he killed Amanda—once he glared forward, harshly, cold and unsympathetic. Now he smiles at them, with a kindness I can't offer those people. He's forgiven their hisses, the mass of them.

I cannot. I will not. I want to fight back. I want to scream at them. I want to scream at myself for being so weak. What's happening to me?

I gasp and touch my cheeks, noticing they're wet with tears. Shit. Focus Avery. Control your goddamn thoughts. Why is this so hard? I return to my happy place, meditating. Remembering what it was like a few short months ago.

Eyes shut tight, I grip the edge of the chair and push back into the pillow further. Deep breaths slow my frantic mind, the worry that claws at my throat. I see it. The waves. They're deep blue, sliding in and out, against the silvery sand. The inky sky to the west is shrinking back as the eastern sky blooms with shades of violet and indigo.

This is my spot. This place beyond the dune, where the water meets the shore, at the end of the world. If the Earth was flat, this is where it begins. This is where the sun creeps over the horizon spilling pots of gold and amber light. The sweet scent of the night air lifts as the waves slink up closer to me, nearing my toes at the edge of the water. The tide is shifting. Soon there will be a sandbar out there covered with life.

The muscles in my arms relax as my breathing slows. In my mind, I'm there. Safe from the thing that frightens me the most.

Me.

CHAPTER 2

A firm, warm hand rests on my shoulder. The touch is firm but soft. Reassuring and possessive. The daydream shatters as I glance up into those vivid sapphire eyes. "Are you hungry?" Sean asks. "I made you something."

I nod and start to push myself up, but Sean reaches out to me, offering me his hand. "Let me help."

I mutter, "I wish you could." Before I know it, I'm standing in his arms, round belly pressed to his flat, toned stomach. I can feel the curve of his muscles, the strength of him through his soft T-shirt. Black. With dark jeans that are slashed and frayed at the knee.

His lips are by my ear, "Tell me. I want to be here for you, Avery, but you've grown so quiet since we got home. It's like someone flipped a switch and turned you off." Still holding me by my upper arms, he pulls away, his eyes roving my face looking for answers. A soft smile lines his lips as he reaches for a stray curl and pushes it behind my ear.

The knot in my throat is massive. I can't breathe. What am I supposed to say? That I managed to tackle the task I set out for when I met him? He'll blame himself. I can't say that. Shrugging, I sigh. Tipping my head to the side, I lie, "I'm just tired."

"When did you see Chan?"

My gaze evades his, eyes dodging everywhere. He gently tugs my chin back toward him. Waiting for an answer that I'm slow to give. "I don't know. Last week, I guess. Everything's blurring together, Sean."

My rigidness is cracking, splintering apart under his gaze. I can't hold myself together much longer. I try to twist out of his grip, saying, "Let's eat on the couch, okay?" But he doesn't release me.

"Avery," he speaks my name like a command. "You will never be the person you were before all this happened. That girl is gone. You know that, but I can't help but feel that Chan has somehow convinced you that you can regain that piece of you if you follow her rules. You can't. God knows I've tried."

Tears spring up in my eyes. Our gazes are locked. "I feel so broken. Everywhere I look is another reminder of the life I lost. Some days I can barely breathe. If it weren't for them..." My hand rests on the swell of my stomach, on the twins growing inside me. My lips remain parted but there are no more words. I don't know how to say it. To tell him what I feel.

The corners of his mouth twitch. There's a moment where he says nothing and then cups both my cheeks, his voice drops an octave with the seriousness of what he's saying. "I know. I see it in you. There's a place for numbness, Avery. A time to use it. And a time to put it away."

"The darkness that was in you, it's gone, Sean. I'm afraid if I go that way, I won't come back." My lower lip is trembling. A bitter laugh is forced from my lungs and sounds like a bark. "Imagine a mother who feels nothing for her baby. Do you want that to be me? If I don't keep fighting, it will be."

Coldness drips down my spine before the words break apart like shards of ice. My throat tightens as I realize how much that thought scares me. My chest rises and falls swiftly as my heart beats out of control like I'm running from Vic through the marshes.

"Avery," his voice is deep, calm. Sean's fingers push back into my hair as he breathes in slowly, surely. He does it again and I copy him, sucking in air as slowly as I can. Trying to calm down.

His dark lashes are lowered, considering his words. When he meets my gaze, he says softly, "This is your path and the pain you feel is because that path is diverging and you've not chosen which way to go. I want you to do whatever you need to do to feel whole again. If that means walking in the shadows, do it. If that means fighting them off, then fight. I just think there's a part of you that's screaming to be heard and it won't be silenced. Until you confront the crux of the matter, you'll never be able to rest. Your life will be a fight where you're railing against it."

I pull away and wrap my arms around my middle, or try to. The bump is a large curve now, so I tuck my arms up under my chest. Head hung low, ice licks its way up my spine. Reforming. Always beckoning. I repress a shudder. Speaking through a wall of curly brown hair, I breathe, "You'll lose me if I stop fighting."

His voice is close. I feel his breath on my neck when he speaks. "I'll never lose you. This is part of you. The part that you're denying. A part that I've already seen. Avery, I know what you've done. You're not weak."

I shake my head, "I am."

"No, you're not," he grabs my shoulders and whirls me toward him. His voice is earnest and his words rapid. "You're trying to deny half of your being. You're not all rainbows and glitter anymore. You've killed people. Nothing removes that stain. It clings and darkens."

"And that's horrible."

"Maybe, but it's also inert. The dark part of you has no power over you. It's like trying to repress laughter because being happy is wrong. It's part of you now. The good and the bad. Let yourself become whoever it is you're meant to be. I won't leave you and I'll never stop loving you."

The quivering in my lower lip returns tenfold. He hit the mark. The sore spot. He said what worries me most. I blink away the layer of tears that haven't fallen from my eyes and hold his gaze. My voice is barely a breath, "You won't?"

"Never." The word rings with absolute

conviction. Sean tips his head to the side, keeping his eyes locked on mine. His sincerity is not pity. It's not gentle either. He's not lied to me and padded what's happening here. If anything, he holds up a metaphorical mirror to make me face it.

"There are times in life," he explains, "that you have to walk through, in utter darkness. You can't force it to stop. You can't take a bypass around it. That's just the way it is. Be who you are now. I think you'll feel better once you—" he stops suddenly. Those sapphire eyes still locked on mine.

"Once I, what? Say it, Sean." My brows are pinched together. This conversation is two parts anxiety and one part brutal honestly. It's hard to swallow.

His lips part as he traces a finger along my cheek. He works his jaw as if he's considering pulling back, not saying whatever he planned, but then I feel the change in him. That he thinks it's better said than left in silence.

"Avery," he takes my hands and dips his head as he speaks. Dark hair falls into his eyes. "Once you stop trying to be someone that no longer exists."

That does it. The tears flow. The ugly sobs start. Before Sean can get his arms around me, I collapse back into the chair, head in hands, hiding my face. He said everything I needed to hear. He gave me the permission I needed to walk on to whatever's next. To feel however I want to feel. To stop looking backward. His strong arms wrap around me as he huddles my body close to his.

"Avery, I love you. Forever. Always. No matter what happens. You're mine."

ays roll by, one after the next. They no longer bleed together at the edges. I do what I want. I no longer want to wear the bright happy maternity clothing, so Sean takes me to a specialty boutique nestled into an alley on the other side of the city. I glance around nervously when the car drops us off and pull my pink polka dot sweater tighter around my body.

Sean sees my unease and laughs. "I know the owner. I promise we're in the right place."

I nod and take his hand as we walk up to a matte black door with a curve at the top. It looks like it once belonged on a church. There's not a bit of luster on it, just thick planks of black wood with the ancient grain exposed. Iron nail heads form a line across the planks. Gothic details are the only decoration. A spindly dragon is perched on an old-fashioned peephole that swings open like a door for a mouse. The dragon's body twists around the tiny opening, his form carved with exquisite detail.

It's not until Sean pulls it open that I realize the thickness and heft of the door. He holds it for me, gesturing for me to enter. I duck under his arm and stop directly on the other side of the doorway. "Uh, Sean?"

His deep chuckle is in my ear as he stands next to me and takes my hand. His eyes shift to the black walls filled with leather straps and harnesses. A red corset is on a black French form under a spotlight by the wall. It's made of straps of blood-red leather, crisscrossing the form, leaving certain things exposed, and it's covered in silver rings. The display has a chain attached to the ring between the breasts of the form that ties off on the wall.

I grip Sean's hand harder. "What are we doing here? I can't do this stuff now."

A devilish smile flashes across his face before he scoffs. "Of course, you can. Unless you're spotting again?" He watches me carefully. I shake my head. Nerves fill my belly and I clutch his hand harder. That deep laugh returns. He stops and tips his head at me, grinning. "Do you really think I'd bring my pregnant wife to an S&M club?"

"Uh, you did." I lift my palm in the air to show off the weird stuff on the other wall and the half-naked couples doing things on that side of the room. I didn't see them until that moment. There was a half wall and too many pillows obstructing our view. My face burns with a fierce blush.

"The owner can make you anything you want," Sean states simply. "Dresses, pants, jackets—whatever."

"How do you know her?" Curiosity gets the better of me.

Sean lifts a dark brow. "Black had a place like this, years ago, before she switched to the operation you stumbled into. The seamstress that worked there owns this place. It's a shop, not an Orgy Fest. I don't know what's up with them." He tips his head at the couples in the corner.

"Wait, Black had a club? You went to it?" My

questions go unanswered as he pulls me deeper into the dimly lit room. "Sean—?"

"I'll fill you in later." Sean walks in long strides up to the desk and rings the bell.

The hum of a machine stops and the place is filled with silence. A moment later, a woman dressed in black with a floor-length black duster emerges from behind a jacquard curtain dividing the front of the shop from her back room. Her lips twist into something of a smile. "Sean Ferro."

"Bella Noir." Sean reaches out and shakes her hand as she leans in and kisses his cheek.

I suppress a giggle. There's no way that's her real name. There are people walking around who have been bestowed names odd and old, but she's not one of them. I can tell. It's part of this place, she's presenting a character. The woman is slender, taller than me with inky hair and cherry stained lips that have perfectly outline bows. The paleness of her skin has caused her to age well, but there are laugh lines on her long face and slight creases by her brown eyes. I suspect she's in her mid-forties.

Bella steps out from behind the counter and ditches the duster on top of it. She presses her hands in front of a Donna Reed-style dress complete with poufy petty coat and apron. The entire outfit is layers of black, an ink colored blouse with ebony buttons trimmed with charcoal lace down the front and tucked into a wide stone colored belt. A thick, black on black striped circle skirt stopped just below the knee. Coupled with black stockings and heels, she seems like an emo Stepford wife. There's a shock of white hair extending from a pointy widow's peak. It's twisted into her victory curls, pinned to her head, with a loose ponytail hanging in the back.

She eyes me wearily, then my bump. "And who is this?"

"This is my wife," Sean says it with pride. "And the reason we came here is that you're the best and she requires something a little different. We need it fast." Sean practically growls the words.

Sean's old demeanor donned like a suit. Oddly enough, it still fits him. That swagger, the roughness to him coupled with the icy eyes speaks volumes. It finally dawns on me that, while I can see a softer side to Sean, he can still flip to dark mode. There is no apprehension while he does it either. Sean's lean body is poised, rigid, one hip against the black counter with the gray granite top. His other arm is wrapped around my waist, holding me like his possession.

Bella cocks her head to the side, places a

manicured hand on her waist. "Well, then, let's get started. Exactly what are you looking for? You know my specialty lies more toward macabre than," she pauses and flicks a dark eyebrow high as she eyes my outfit, then returns her gaze to Sean, "that."

"Maternity stores don't have what she's looking for. We want an entire wardrobe. Whatever she wants." Sean's voice is firm, but I feel the warmth of his hand on my back.

"Sean, I can't—" I glance at him, not sure what he expects me to get here.

"You should dress how you feel. You're not polka dots and cute right now. You're a badass. You're a survivor. You're someone not to fuck with. The fact that your pregnant doesn't change that. What would you be wearing if you weren't with child?"

I smirk. Sean flips to formal mode sometimes, like he's at prep school. "I don't know. Black. Leather. Thigh high boots. A thick jacket. Nothing bright. And not that." I point at Bella's outfit.

Bella slips her tongue over her teeth revealing a silver barbell before she laughs softly. "What crawled up your ass, honey?" She glances at Sean and lowers her false lashes and smiles with those huge painted lips. "Oh, right. I'd be bent out of shape too."

Sean gives Bella a look that makes her retreat behind the counter, but I don't want him defending me. Something inside the foggy mess of my mind sparks to life. "Listen. I get it, I'm just not into that—"

"Era?" Bella says surely, her neck long and her chin up. Proud.

"No, beavers. You may use that whole *Leave it to Beaver* outfit as a calling card, but that's not what I want." I feel feisty. I think pregnancy hormones are making me bitchy but I'm not totally certain since Sean is suppressing a grin.

Bella snorts. Touches a hand to her hair. "Then what do you want, Barbie? Because I'm not here to play dress up with the knocked-up version of Rainbow Brite."

I laugh. Loud and hard. It makes me wince and put a hand on my belly. I glance at Sean, "Anything?"

"Go for it." He backs up and lifts himself onto the counter, legs hanging over the edge. "Leather, suede, knit, lace, whatever you want, she can make."

A smile spills across my lips. There's a strange ache like I've not used those muscles in a long time. I rub my palms together and walk over to Bella, "Come on emo Mary Poppins. Let's get this baby mama feeling more like herself."

Bella eyes me, her lips in a crooked grin, before she glances back at Sean. "It'll cost you, Ferro."

He lifts a hand, waving her off. "I wouldn't expect any less of you."

CHAPTER 4

SUNDAY AFTERNOON

It's strange how clothes can make you feel like you. Or someone else. Someone completely different. The happy crap from the maternity stores was strangling me. It's not that I'm not excited about the babies. I am. It's just I don't know how to live this life I've been thrust into. There's a permanently damaged part of me, and I have no idea what to do with it. But it rears its head and vomits at pink polka dots and ruffles. Whoever decided that pregnant women all wanted to look round and cute was insane.

This is a million times better. More me. A mix of past and present. Darkness and light. At first, I was hesitant but Bella made a few suggestions. Take this in here, let that out there. Combine this fabric with this metallic thread. I'm hooked. I didn't know clothing could be so customized. It's not just, "put these shoes with this skirt." No, my outfits are as different as Bella's emo Betty Crocker get-up.

A few alterations later, and I've found my new look. Freedom from cute and perky. Bella altered a few pieces while I was in her shop. My favorite, the one I'm wearing now, was a full-length black croqueted corset. It originally stretched from bust to hip, but Bella cut it off above the waist, just under the bust, right above the swell of the baby bump. Other things were done to increase comfort and my everchanging body. She replaced the steel boning with plastic, added thick elastic side panels, and cut away some of the stiff fabric. Those flexible panels are hidden by my arms, but the texture change on the sides is interesting to look at too. It's pretty. In a badass way.

Bella made the corset curve easier to my figure. I don't feel crushed like I did the last time I wore one of these. Finally, Bella added a stiff seam to the hem so the plastic boning won't jab into the babies. She pulled the leather straps used to lace the back of the corset and replaced it with a metallic silver ribbon. Two pieces of lace were tacked onto the shoulders, making a cap sleeve at the top of each arm. No ruffle.

The way she made this outfit will accommodate me up until I have the babies and then after. She also said a corset will feel good after they're born, so I ordered a long-waisted one for later.

Bella shoves a pencil behind her ear, and tugs at the measuring tape around her neck as she looks over her creation. There's a knowing smirk on her lips as if she already knows what I'll say. There's a confident tone in her voice when she asks, "Well? What do you think?"

I'm barefoot in her back room wearing the modified corset with an A-line skirt that flares above the knee. There's a pair of gray and white Chucks on the chair behind me, the type that laces up the calf all the way to the knee. There's a long silver streak up the back of the heel. It glitters slightly.

Pressing my lips together, I repress a smile as I glance in the mirror, then at the sneakers. The woman in the mirror isn't the old me. She's not the Avery that never knew Sean. That girl is gone. At the same time, she's not the new me either. I've landed somewhere in between. It's "Preggers Avery" with a dash of darkness and a smidgen of glitter. I'm an emo pregnancy unicorn. The thought cracks the smile across my face.

"Fuck, yeah. Called it." Bella raises her hands in the air and then snaps.

Grudgingly, I nod. "Yeah, fine. You nailed it. One look in the mirror and I want more. This is amazing. I twist at the waist and I'm not stuck. The garment moves with me. I can move! And...this," I run my fingers over the corseted top, tracing the slick dark fabric. "I love it."

Bella grunts with approval. "Good, then let's take care the rest of this. Just because you're pregnant doesn't mean you need to ignore all that." She gestures toward my bottom.

I look down at the skirt that's hiding my huge granny panties and frown. "No one makes pretty maternity panties."

"I do." Her dark eyebrow climbs up on one side as she folds her arms over her chest. She sighs and lifts a finger, pointing at the undies beneath the skirt. "And you'll burn those as soon I get my knickers to you."

"If they can deal with the bump and my ever-growing ass, sure. But if they don't stay put and crawl all over the place—" I'm making a face as I relive some sexy items Sean bought me before the babies came into the picture.

Bella scoffs, "Nothing will crawl all over you unless you want it to. So, butterfly, crotchless, tear away, snaps?"

"What?" I stare at the woman like she has two head.

"Oh, dear God." Bella pinches the bridge of her nose for a second before sucking in a deep breath and then looking up at me with a deranged grin. "I'll make a mixed lot for you."

Raising a finger, I open my mouth to tell her that function outranks form, but she cuts me off.

"I know. Comfort and function are musts."

After that, we went back into the supply room where she had bolts of fabric in a million shades of black to dark gray. I point at a few and then she takes a few more bolts of fabric from below the counter. As she piles them up on her workspace, she snatches a bolt of leather, takes her sheers, and cuts off a piece. A few measurements later and I'm wearing a leather A-line skirt. It's high waisted so it bumps up against the corset top. She pulls a pair of Mary Janes with silver tipped toes and slips my feet into them.

"What about the Chucks?" I ask.

Bella shrugs. "These are for when you can't stand the thought of lacing those up."

Peering down at my silver-toed shoe, I twist it one way and then the other. A smile spills across my lips. Perfection. The clothing matches my mood. I can move. I can breathe. I feel dark and light. Maybe a bit shiny. And it's okay.

$\mathcal{S}$ ean's fingers are laced through mine as we walk down the street. "Goth pregger chick" and a Ferro. Life as it's meant to be. The corset has my boobs so high that it makes my figure look super curvy. I feel like a goddess even though I'm stretched and have a round belly poking forward. The skirt drapes over the twins, showing them off rather than concealing them with ruffles or pleats. I left my hair loose, long dark curls hanging down my back.

Sean looks me over, squeezes my hand before saying, "You seem like you feel a little better."

I nod. "I do. Thank you. I was a little concerned when we first went in there."

He laughs. "I know. I saw your face."

I bump him with my shoulder, but he doesn't move. The man is a wall of muscle. Repressing a grin, I squeeze his hand harder, jerk his arm a bit. Then I lean in and whisper, "I can't believe you can still surprise me."

"I can't believe you can't believe it." Sean laughs. It's that rich deep sound that makes me want to curl into him and never let go. "We tend to shock the hell outta each other."

I snort. "Nice grammar, Mr. Prep School. So, what'd you do while Bella was sewing this outfit?"

"I went shopping for myself, made a few calls."

"Calls?" I stop walking and stand in the middle of the city sidewalk. The sun is setting and it's getting chilly.

"That's the part you want to ask about?" Sean stops, turning toward me as he rubs his hands up and down my arms. "Really? You don't want to ask if I engaged with the orgy couples? Or what I bought?"

I smirk up at him. His eyes don't stray. I've noticed. I humor him. "Did you join them?"

His sapphire eyes bore into mine. "No. I have exactly what I want."

Swallowing hard, I nod. My teeth graze my lower lip, feeling that more is coming as we start walking again, his fingers thread with mine. "And the phone call?"

He swings our hands as a playful grin spreads across his face. "To Dr. Liz."

I stop suddenly, lurching him around to face me. "Why?"

"I wanted to see if it would be safe for you to do certain things. I was given guidelines, assurances, and told specific directions. The doctor gave me her cell number too."

I frown at him, feeling my cheeks heat. "What did you ask her that would make her give you her number?"

He shrugs. "Nothing. I was completely honest." He leans forward and presses his lips to my ear, whispering what he told her—the things he wants to do to me.

Jaw flapping, I step back and giggle, shoving him in the chest and then turning to walk away as nonsensical words tumble out of my mouth. I gape at him. "You said that! To her?"

He nods. "Why not?"

"Because!" I shove his chest again.

"Your face is bright red, badass. Are you embarrassed?" Sean chuckles as his gaze sweeps over me, taking in my reaction.

"No!" It's a huge lie. I'm dying inside. I want to cover my face and hide under a sewer cap. Maybe after we do the things he asked about. I glance up at him from between my fingertips. "Well?"

Sean laughs, those dark lashes lowering as he examines me. As he steps toward me, he rests his hands on my waist, "Well, what Miss Smith?"

The smile on my face is so big that it's going to eat my head. "You know, what! Tell me what she said."

People around us stop and stare. A camera flash goes off as a paparazzo steals a shot of us. He doesn't run this time. The guy lingers as he should, but his camera hovers by his eye, ready to grab another picture should the moment arise.

Sean gives him the picture, let's the guy take the shot. Sean leans in and kisses my cheek. His arms around my waist, hands resting on my belly. Those warm luscious lips pressed to my cheek. My hands are on top of his, lashes lowered, face still crimson. The bit of wind that blows lifts my hair and the flash goes off. When I look up, the guy with the camera is gone.

I glance at Sean. "You did that on purpose."

"I did no such thing." He's so close that I can feel his warmth. We're toe-to-toe on a city side-walk. Even though there are people around, it feels intimate.

"Yes, you did," I insist. Sean's a breath away now. Inching closer to my face, his eyes locked on my lips. "You gave him that shot."

"Maybe. Maybe I wanted it." Those blue eyes dart up and meet mine. He lifts a brow and confesses, "I refuse to use a selfie stick."

I honk out a laugh, pressing my hands to my belly. Tears form at the edges of my eyes as I feel a tiny foot brush my ribs. I finally smile up at him again. "So, tell me. What did she say?"

Sean leans in close. "The doc said yes."

This time the blush spreads to consume my entire body.

CHAPTER 6

We meander back to the penthouse. I'm feeling better than usual, less like a floundering crazy person. I hope it doesn't vanish, so I try to live in the moment and not think about anything else.

Sean takes care of dinner, working in the kitchen. The smell fills the place, finally reaching me back in the bedroom where I'm sitting on a leather chair, reading a book. The scent lures me from the room. I've kicked off the shoes and stockings, but I still have on the half corset and skirt. Padding down the hallway, I find Sean in the kitchen with an apron tucked tightly around his narrow waist, holding a saucepan. He tips it to the side, spilling the contents over a bed of noodles.

My mouth waters. "Oh my God, is that what I think it is?"

"Fettuccini and veal scaloppini. Just for you." He flicks his gaze up and holds mine, a smile spreads across his lips. "Plus, a little bottle of baby-friendly booze."

"Really?" He nods, pointing toward a bag on the counter as he dishes up the food.

"It smells so good." I want to lick the pan right now. I open the brown paper bag on the counter and look inside. There's a pink shiny bottle. It's a mini champagne bottle. "What is this?"

"It's a non-alcoholic rosé sparkling apple cider."

"Where'd you find it?" I try to open the bottle and can't, so I just walk it to the table and put it down.

"This is New York. You can find anything if you look." Sean carries out two plates of food, that apron still tucked around his waist. He looks so good and I haven't been with him for a while. I miss the feel of his skin beneath my hands. He glances up at me. "Sit."

I practically orgasm over the food. It's light and delicious. Oddly, the cider is perfectly paired with the meal. Sean has some too, skipping his usual scotch. When we've finished eating, he watches me, his eyes dipping to the corset top. "Is that comfortable? I'm surprised you didn't take it off right away."

I rip off a piece of bread and pop it in my mouth. Nodding, I confess, "Yeah, I didn't think I'd be able to wear it like this. It's like a sports bra but has more support. Lifts instead of smooshing." I smile and glance up at him. "I love it. This was a great gift. Thank you."

"I bought you something else today." He lifts a bag with Bella's logo on it. Puts it on the table.

I press my lips together and lift my eyes to meet his. Heart pounding, I ask, "Is this what you asked the doctor about?"

"Yes."

"And you want to do this tonight?"

He leans forward, intense, and takes my hand. "If you want to."

The truth is, I don't know what I want. I'm angry. I haven't wanted to do something where I took it out on him by accident. I'm suddenly looking at the wall, avoiding his gaze.

"Avery, tell me." His words are kind. An invitation.

Lifting my lashes, I glance back at him and

confess. The swirl of emotions is so unpredictable. The anger. The rage. It's not gone. "I don't want to hurt you or the baby. I don't want to lose control because I don't know what I'll do."

He nods slowly, steepling his fingers together. Watches me, considers his words, and says, "Look in the bag and then tell me your answer. We can find something else to do. Or you can choose that. It's your call. I won't push you."

Hesitantly, I reach for the bag and pull it toward me. I reach in and feel several sensations—silk, leather, wood. I pull out items one at a time and turn them over in my hands. Leather cuffs with chains. Silk ribbons. A soft blindfold. A feather duster made with fine soft down. Shimmering powder. And a bundle of straps. The spot between my legs is warm from just talking about this.

Breathing hard, I shake my head. "I don't think I can let you tie me down right now. It'll make me worse. I'll—"

Sean leans forward, takes my hands under his. "No. Not you. Me."

"What?" I blink at him as if I can't believe what he's offering.

He presses his lips together and parts his hands before placing them on the table. "Anything you want. You're in control. Use me any way you want, Avery." Sean's voice is caught between a whisper and a plea.

There's a deafening silence that devours the room. Suddenly, I'm aware of my fingers, my hands, and the way my skin prickles as if I'm frozen. This offer is extremely unlike Sean. Based on everything he told me, this is an offer he'd never have made when we first met. But then many things have changed since then.

Clearing my throat, I put down my fork, and grab my sparkling cider. Holding it between us makes me feel like I have a little bit of a buffer. Although I know I'm treading into unknown territory and it's equal parts frightening and alluring. The click of my fork on the table top seems to echo.

Nervously, I shift in my chair and glance at him through my lashes as I ask softly, "I don't understand. I thought you needed to be in control. I thought—"

Cutting me off, Sean replies with a tentative smile, like he's uncertain of this conversation. The bluster, the arrogance that straightens his spine and sparks in his gaze is gone. Clearing his throat, he opens his mouth and closes it. Head tipping to the side, he starts again, but no words come out. There's a flash of a smile, of straight white teeth, before he shakes his head.

Reaching out, I press my hand to the table. I can't quite reach him. Stupid extra long table. Constance doesn't want anyone touching at family dinners. This table is the size of a bed. While we are sitting across from each other instead of at the ends, he's still not close enough to touch with more than my fingertips. His eyes lock onto the movement, staring at my hand.

I breathe, "You can tell me. Anything." My fingers are there, barely out of reach of Sean's hand.

He leans across the table, getting closer to me, and presses his hand over mine. "I know what I said in the past."

"Did that change?" My eyebrow climbs up, hides under curled bangs that are overgrown and no longer straightened. The room feels like it's tilting so I move with it, tipping my head to the side, trying to catch his gaze, but Sean doesn't look up.

There are no words. Only jagged breaths and the sound of my heart slamming into my ribs. It stretches on for miles, spanning the distance between us. Making me feel like I'm a million miles away. Guilt gnaws at me for leaving him alone for so long. Sean offers snuggles, hugs, back rubs, and everything I could ever ask for and more. I didn't think about him, not with this. Not with sex. I assumed it had to disappear for a time. It was a stupid assumption compounded by lethargy and morning sickness. Yet, Sean still smiles at me, holds my hand, and acts like intimacy hasn't left us. I swallow hard when I realize it has and that it's my fault. I should have told him.

The little voice inside my head brushes against my mind. *Talk to him. Ask him. Be there for him. You don't have to leave him alone.*

Before I can speak, Sean's lips part. He confesses so softly that I can barely hear him. "Nothing changed in that regard." Slowly, he lifts his head, his dark hair falling forward into his eyes. He brushes it away as his azure eyes lock on mine. They widen as if he's realized something. He scoots to the edge of his chair, moving closer to me and stretches his arm across the table so he can rub his thumb along the back of my hand. His touch lingers, the rough skin on his thumb swirling a pattern on the back of my palm.

"I've changed." A confession. His brow pulls tight as he attempts to say the words buried deep within. "I was a different person when I met you. I needed that fear, that flicker of panic from you."

"And now?"

He shakes his head. "No. I mean, it's still

intoxicating to be with you, to rule your body in that capacity..." his voice trails off. "Part of me is still shocked it ever happened."

I smile at him. "Me too."

Sean inhales deeply and pulls his hands back, places them on the sides of his head and then runs his fingers through his hair, pushing it back from his eyes. When his hands reach his neck, they linger there. The pose is open and completely vulnerable. "It's just—I need you. I know there will be times you can't—that we can't be together. And I'll protect you and the children with every ounce of my being, Avery."

CHAPTER 7

I can't help it. I smile so wide that I feel like a fool. Wattage is turned up to stare at the sun intensity as my soul beams with love and pride. The fact that he can confess anything to me is miles from where we started. But this. This is one of those rare moments where time slows down and the choice I make here will change my life. Our lives. I feel it. Sense it.

I have trouble not talking over him, giving

him the time to say what he wants without derailing him so I bite my lower lip and listen.

"I've put a lot of thought into this, Avery. This way the babies are safe, and you can—" he swallows so hard his Adam's apple shifts in his throat. Sean pulls back his hands.

I latch on, lacing my fingers between his, pressing my belly into the edge of the table. I'm not about to let this go. We've not been together in a few weeks. He's not pressured me at all. I was waiting for the doctor to give permission. I didn't want to risk the baby. Babies. I still can't fathom that there are two babies. Inhaling deeply, I release "I can what?"

There's silence as if we're approaching a subject that he doesn't want to unveil. The strength of his hands is warm. He squeezes once and releases me. Stands. Walks to the kitchen, speaking over his shoulder. His lips curl into an awkward smile. "Never mind. It's not the right time for this."

The hell it's not. I jump up from my seat and pad barefoot across the floor, at his heels. "You don't know that. Ask me. Say it, Sean." There's a demanding tone in my voice. It's not desperation or anything like that. It's the plea of one partner wanting to support the other. For the life of me, I can't fathom where this conversation is going. "Sean?"

He doesn't turn. "It's nothing."

"Don't do that. It's something important. I'm not that addle-brained, not yet anyway. Tell me. I won't judge." It can't be weirder than the things we've already done. Although I can't fathom what he wants to do to me that won't risk the babies and still is sexually satisfying for him—for us. There's been an element of danger in many of our trysts. Since I told him about the pregnancy, he's not broached the subject of tanks or boxes. Part of me is glad. But in some ways, it's sad.

When Sean doesn't reply, I hedge, "I want you to want me. I know this isn't exactly sexy," I rub a hand over my growing belly, "but I—"

He rounds on me, his body coiled with tension and a look in his eye that threatens to devour me. His hands are on my forearms as his gaze pins me in place. His words are sharp, pointed so that they directly hit my soul. "You are the most beautiful, sexy, alluring woman I've ever seen. Pregnancy has only made those things that attracted me to you more so. I can't stop looking at you, wanting you. Avery, I love the curve here," two of his fingers trace the line of my growing abdomen, "the way the world knows I adore you, fuck you, and those babies are mine. You're as sexy as you've ever been. You're mine."

His hands tangle in my hair as he holds my head in place, making sure I look into his eyes as he confesses these things. Part of it is carnal, the display of the ramifications of sex, the swell of my breasts and belly. There's pride gleaming in his eyes. Every magazine focuses on getting my body back in shape so he'll want me again after the pregnancy. They mention sagging skin, stretched and ruined. The way Sean is looking at me now speaks another story.

There's a tremor at the corners of my mouth. I don't know if I should smile or cry. "You really believe that?"

Those lips. His delicious, velvety smooth mouth tips up at one corner, giving me a beautiful smile. "It's not a belief. That's the reality of our situation." His hands slip down my curves and rest on my hips. His eyes dart between my lips and eyes. He'll kiss me and I'll forget what he wanted to tell me because this wasn't it. I derailed him with my own insecurities.

Standing on my tippy toes, I splay my hands on his chest, across that soft black shirt, and press my breasts and belly against his taut body. God, I miss him. "Tell me. Say whatever it was you wanted to say. Please."

I feel his breath hitch and I swear his heart fell down a staircase, tumbling with each rapid thud. Or maybe that's my pulse, freaking out.

What could be worse than that tank? Or the box?

Sean holds me close and finally confesses what he wants. "Things change. I know they do. And in your condition, we can't partake in certain activities. So, I was thinking we should reverse roles."

"I don't understand." I pull back from him a little and look up into his beautiful face. "What do you mean?"

Sean swallows hard as if his mouth has gone dry. His jaw is tight and it takes a tremendous amount of effort for him to free the words. "What if you take out your emotions on me? Use me. Fully. I'm yours, Avery."

When I try to pull my hands away, he restrains me. My gaze drops to the empty plates on the table. The conversation we had over the meal is long forgotten. My eyes jump from the feathers to the silks, to the leather straps. He wants me to reverse things. Tie him up and be rough with him.

Am I that person? Can I cross that line? For some reason, I don't think I have, but I don't remember it. Not like this. Not taking full possession of Sean and doing anything and everything.

Fear claws its way up my throat because I don't want to be soft with him. I want the harshness, the brutality of carnal love, raw and unsated. Oh my God. I can't.

Jerking my hands out of his, I shake my head. "No. This isn't…" I can't say it.

Sean stands with me, remains at arm's length like he's worried I'll run. "You don't have to do anything. Avery." I glance up at him when he says my name, pulled from the images he's laced within my mind. "It was just a suggestion. The other option is this." He lifts the bundle of leather straps with ropes on two spots.

"What is that?"

"A swing. I can hold you, cuddle you, gently make love to you without hurting you." He reaches for me, strokes his hand in my hair. "We can have the softness. We can snuggle and throw this thing out. Whatever you want. I miss you and thought you may want to try it."

"Why does it feel like you're pushing me down the dark path?"

Sean pulls away and speaks sharply. "I'm not making you do anything."

"But you are. You are, Sean. Why? I feel like you should tell me. I'm not a china doll. I won't break because you say something mean. Just say whatever it is you're thinking." It's not a fight. Not yet. But the floor feels uneven. Like I should tread carefully.

"Avery, you're already on the dark path.

Okay? That's it. That's what I see. I know because I've been there and denying it just makes it harder."

"So, you want me to beat you? Is that what you think will make me feel better? I'm not angry at you!" My voice is loud. I'm yelling and I don't know why. I'm angry and I have no idea where to direct it. It's not Sean though. I know that much. He saved me. I suck in a jagged breath and hiss through my teeth, "This is wrong."

Sean shakes his head. "It's only wrong if neither of us wants it. If one person forces it on the other. I know where you are and what you need. Why won't you take it?"

I shake my head and step away. Wrapping my arms around my middle, I retreat further into the living room. My jaw is clenched shut, shoulders tight. I'm so rigid I can barely breathe. "I'm not her."

"Who?" Sean steps toward me, his gaze searching for mine, but I won't look at him.

"You can't make me." My eyes burn, but tears don't fall. "I'm not her. I won't become her."

Hands are on my shoulders, fingers on my chin, and then he lifts it so I have to look him in the eye. "Who? Say what you're thinking. Tell me."

"Black." I didn't realize what was going through my mind until it tumbled out of my mouth.

"Black?"

"Yes!" I pull away from him, shaking him off. "She's depraved. Sex isn't love to her. It's recreation, intimidation, manipulation, and a million other ways to crush someone. I'm not her." My spine straightens as I look him in the eye. "I won't become her."

Silence fills the air. Sean remains distant and slips his hands into his pockets. "I never thought you were like her at all. The two of you are incomparable. I didn't realize you were worried about this."

Neither did I. I glance at him out of the corner of my eye and repress a shiver. There's a tidal wave of thoughts burning through my brain. They're so close to spilling over my lips. Arms wrapped tightly around my middle, I glance over at him. "Have you let anyone do anything like this to you before?"

He nods once.

"Who?" I regret asking, but the question is already out of my mouth.

"It's not Black if that's what you want to know. It was a long time ago. It was brutal. There was no love there. It's not like this, not like what I'm offering at all." Sean holds my gaze for a long time and then looks away.

He turns toward the couch and falls into the cushions, sitting down swiftly, before pinching the bridge of his nose. "I have a past, Avery. I can't erase it."

"I don't want you to." I'm standing alone in the middle of the room, watching him.

He regrets suggesting this. I can tell. He thinks he pushed me too far, asking me to do something I didn't have any desire to do.

My lips part and I try to say it. I can't watch him blame himself like this. I spit out the words without thinking, not wanting to admit it to myself. Saying it out loud makes it real. I feel it as the words are forced from my body, and hang in the air. "It intrigues me. You're not wrong. Sex, like that. Being the one in control. The carnal rawness of it. Mixing pleasure and pain." I swallow hard and breathe the words, "You're not wrong."

Those sapphire eyes look up at me. His reply is one word, a reprimand. "Don't."

"I'm not," I snap back, offended. "Raking my nails down your back isn't enough sometimes. Sometimes, I want to do more." I stand there like a girl abandoned on an island, confessing something wicked to the wind. My throat is tight thinking about it. Putting the thoughts into pictures in my mind and then voicing them into words.

It's real now. That desire. And he knows. He's known. For how long? It doesn't matter.

There's a pause. Sean asks a careful question, "What do you want to do to me? What have you imagined?"

I shrug and twist my hands in front of me. "I don't know exactly. I just know it's not what we've been doing. I feel listless. It's infuriating. I just want to—" I'm looking at him, at his beautiful face, and thinking about the things I'd do to him if he were tied up. Sean Ferro at my mercy. The roughness that once terrified me is alluring. It's been calling to me and I've been denying it fiercely. But, that's not how a mom acts. That's not who I am, who I was. Torn between allowing that part of me to break free and shoving it back down, I stare at him. Lost in his eyes. Utterly lost.

A nervousness works its way through me. The innate desire is so conflicted that talking about it makes me really uncomfortable. Putting something to words makes it real. But he already knows. He sees it, though I've barely admitted it to myself.

After a moment, eyes on the floor, I swallow hard and add, "You won't think less of me?"

Sean is across the room and in front of me.

There's a rush of air around him as if he were falling toward me. Suddenly he's there, filling the space, making my heart beat harder.

Although he's near, he still doesn't touch me. The space between us fills with the scent of his cologne. Something that's unmistakably intense, dark, and seductive. Like Sean. I feel his eyes on me when he asks, "Did you think less of me for being so brutal with you at times?"

I shake my head and try to ignore the tightness in my throat. Veins of vulnerability shoot out from my heart and spiderweb across my carefully constructed façade. My shoulder lifts a little. A half shrug, as if those times weren't terrifying at first. Tucking a strand of hair behind my ear, I confess, "No, I didn't think less of you. It was scary and enticing. Exciting in a way. I don't know how to describe it. At first, I didn't want it. But now..." I swallow hard, refusing to meet his gaze. The fissures I've created over my carefully contrasted secret are about to break free.

Closer. Somehow, he's closer but not touching. Nose to nose, as if leaning in for a kiss, his voice is a whisper. "So, what's holding you back?"

The words are so raw, so clenched down,

that they rip my throat as I force them out. "I don't know."

If I say the truth, I can't take it back. I'll have to admit that this part of me, the dark part, the anger—it's there and I let it take over. It tastes like a failure, but no matter how hard I push the feelings away, they keep coming back.

We stand toe-to-toe watching each other. Neither of us speaks. The tension between us is corded tight like a rubber band about to break. I want his hands on me, I want to feel the strength of his touch coupled with the possessive warmth. I don't want the softness, the "please" and "thank you" of it all. I want to feel him take my face between his palms so I can do the same. I want to tip his lips to mine, and thread my fingers through his hair, pull hard and control the kiss. A ferocity I don't recognize burns within me. Lust for devouring him whole, and taking what I want from him.

My lashes lower, fanning across my cheek, as I try to remain in control. Simmer down. But thinking of his lips and the way they lock on mine. The taste of his mouth. The way I could press his back to the wall and press my body against him. The thought of that hot kiss is all consuming. There's no part of me that doesn't respond when he's this close, a breath away. The steady pounding of my heart increases as my body heats. What would I do to him? If he was truly vulnerable, unable to escape—is that really appealing to me?

When I spit out the words, I'm almost laughing at the absurdity of my statement. "I'm not a dominatrix."

"No one is asking you to be." His voice is deep, rich, and utterly sincere. He wants to set me free. I feel it. The way he watches me, the way his eyes bore into me, makes that truth undeniable.

Something deep within my soul calls out to him on a feral level and it scares me. No, it's more than fear. It's terrifying. The thought steals my breath and sends shivers down my spine. I don't know what to do with that rough craving and never have—so I pretended it wasn't there. But standing here now, knowing he won't judge me for it, realizing he wants this part of me. It changes things.

If I believe him. Why is it so hard to accept the truth? Why do I assume everyone prefers lies and pretty words? Especially Sean. That man has never been about sugary words. His bluntness could make me bleed if he chose to unleash his tongue in that manner on me. But he's not. Not now. Not with this. His eyes haven't left my face. The way he searches me, as if he can see through my skin and into my heart still haunts me. I don't look in those places. I can't accept this, so how can he?

That's when I suck in a jagged breath and push past him. I pad over to the table and sit. Sometimes there are no words. But it's my fault this go. Hiding my eyes from him creates a barrier between us. It's wafer-thin, but it's better than his soul-searching stare. I lift my glass and tip back the rest of my cider.

Sean's eyes are on me, but he doesn't say anything. After a few beats, he turns away and walks down the hall. The sound of the shower turning on follows a few moments later.

The tightness around my heart eases and I don't know if I'm relieved or disappointed.

CHAPTER 8

The next morning, neither of us mentions the night before, the confession I almost made. I can't tell if Sean is disappointed or relieved. I'm sitting on the couch in fugly maternity PJs that I thought would look cute, but they just make me feel lost. Pursing my lips, I blow gently on the cup of tea in my hands. The glass is hot and warms my cold fingers. A drape of dark hair falls over my shoulder as I tip my head and look out at the rising city. Amber light spills from the horizon as the sun slowly climbs into the sky. The light slips over the murky darkness littered with lights, casting the city in a heavenly glow.

Sleep was evasive last night. I finally gave up and let Sean have the bed to himself about an hour ago. He didn't follow me. It's almost like he's giving me space, time away that I didn't ask for—I'm not sure I need it. He's annoyingly astute at times. Like with the maternity clothes and the inky part of me that's sucking the glitter out of my veins.

Maybe I don't want to admit that part of me is gone. The piggy kite and the girl laughing on the beach. The girl who wore no coat to let the cold seep in because she wanted to feel something. Now I feel so much I'm trying to block it out. I don't know how to experience this. My life took a weird turn, one I never saw coming. And instead of riding the storm through to the other side, the line to my dingy snapped and I flew out to sea.

Putting my lips to the rim of the mug, I take a sip and savor the heat that runs down my throat. An image of Sean in the shower, of his bottles of body wash, of the things we did— how he tastes—rushes me all at once. I swat at the memories, trying to push them away. The tank. The box. The fear that I once felt has been replaced with something else. I can't tell if it's curiosity or retribution. I'm angry. I know that, but is it that simple? That my dark desires are just because I want payback for a life I can't control? For the times when Sean stole bits of freedom.

Something in my mind snaps at me, denying that, knowing those thoughts aren't true. I want what I want. While rage and anger may be part of it, those feelings aren't because of Sean. So, I shouldn't aim my fury at him. Right?

Sighing, I put my mug on the coffee table in front of me and bury my face in my hands. My hair falls around my face, hiding me from the world. What's my problem? I've already done dark sexual acts with him. Why is it so hard to admit it's me initiating things this time? That I want to control him in bed. That I want the pain and pleasure mix right now. When did Sean turn into a ray of sunshine? It's almost as if we flipped roles in this relationship.

"I didn't hear you leave." Sean's voice is behind me, still addled with sleep.

Startled because I'm too lost in my thoughts, I didn't realize he's there until he speaks. At the sound of his voice, my heart jumps into my throat. My hand flies to my chest as I suck in air. Glancing at him through the wall of hair, I laughingly scold, "You're a goddamn cat, sometimes."

Sean sits down hard on the couch next to me. His hair is tousled and his eyes are still heavy with sleep. There's a toddler-esque lost-ness on his face this early in the morning that I rarely get to see. I wonder if the babies inside me will be wide awake like me in the mornings or take a bit to shake off sleep the way Sean does.

A crooked smile spills across his lips, as he reaches for my tea. His eyes are looking out at the city, as he says in a deep husky voice, "Meow."

A snort escapes me. It's so unexpected that a blaring chortle follows. A smile drips from my lips and fades as fast as it appeared. "I don't know how you do that."

Sean lifts a dark brow as he swallows the tea. His lip curls at the taste before he sets it down again. "I think we need to do something different today."

Sean never drinks tea. Like ever. It was odd he picked it up. "Yeah? Like drink tea or did you think that was coffee?"

He inhales slowly and turns those sapphire eyes my way. A thrill bursts inside of me when he looks at me like that, as if I'm a goddess and he can't look away from me. I shove his shoulder and tuck wayward curls behind my ear. "Stop it."

"What?" He smiles back as if he's not looking at me with sex on his mind. "I'm just wondering why you're dressed all cute instead of wearing the black lace you got from Bella." He yawns and puts his arm around my shoulders, pulling me to him.

"There's a practical issue with some of the pajamas."

"Really? Like what?"

Resting my head against his shoulder, I breathe him in. "It's hard to stay cool in leather. I'm always cold, but at night, I've been too hot lately."

"Mmmm. It's because you're lying next to me." His fingers stroke my hair as I feel a grin lift his cheeks.

"Oh, hot damn. Call the fireman." My voice is light and teasing.

Sean snorts, and asks me, "Really? You like that song?" He lifts his head and examines me as if the awful truth of falling prey to catchy pop music will be the end of us.

"You listen to the Spice Girls when no one is around, so don't judge."

He nods slowly, not denying it. His face is placid, eyes still sleepy when he says, "So tell me what you want, what you really, really want."

I can't help it. I laugh so hard that the joy of

the moment shoots through my entire body, rocking me forward and out of his embrace. As I bust a rib laughing, he sits there, serene. He reaches for me, pushes my hair over my shoulder so the tangle of curls rests on my back.

When I finally stop choking on laughter, I glance over at him, but the giggles take hold. Every time I think of it, I start laughing again.

Sean's voice is flat, deadpan. "If I knew you'd be so responsive to my singing, I would have made more of an effort ages ago."

I fall backward, into him, allowing his arms to envelope me. His warmth surrounds me and, in that moment, I'm not torn, worried, or lost. I'm Avery and he's Sean. And that's enough. A calm settles over us as we cuddle and watch the city come alive on the streets below.

"I love this view." I'm thinking of watching the seasons change from this window. The contrast between black pavement and nature contained to the park across the way is alluring. Asphalt and flowers living side by side, in a weird juxtaposed harmony. There will be flames of orange and crimson on the trees come Autumn. A Christmas tree with twinkling lights in the winter will block the statute of the man on the horse at the park's entrance. Followed by pink blossoms on cherry trees in the spring. Come summer, everything will be lush and green.

"So do I." Sean rest's his head on top of mine. He'd been looking at me. His gaze slides over my body, the curves that grow more pronounced every day.

At times I wonder if he's afraid. He lived through this part of marriage and pregnancy before. My mood swings must be worrisome for him but he never says anything.

It's as if he reads my mind because he says softly, "This is my favorite time of day. It's filled with promise and the newness of life. Even in the winter when everything is stripped clean and there's not a spot of green to be seen. The way the light flows over the buildings, down the streets, and into the park..." his voice trails off and he shrugs. "I don't know. There's just something about it."

"Hope?" My question hangs in the air and he nods slowly, his stubble catching in my hair a little.

"I think so. It's strange."

"What is?"

"I never thought I'd be here, in the city again. Not for this long. With love. With a family. With a wife and babies on the way. I thought my chance at that had passed. I didn't step foot in Manhattan unless I had to."

"I'm glad you did." My mind drifts back to when I first saw him. To the day in the grave-yard. "Grief makes strange lives."

He nods a few times. Then adds, "It paves a path. I had to decide which one to pursue. There were several to choose from, some that would have destroyed me. I thought I didn't deserve this."

"And now you do?" A confession like this from him is rare. I'm assuming it's because of last night, but it could be because things are changing again, for both of us.

He shifts us and pulls away so he can see me. "There's a lack of gratitude in thinking I deserve anything. No, it's not that. It's not that I deserve it. Or earned, hell knows I didn't do that." He grins that perfectly sexy crooked smile and runs his hand through his dark hair, and then over the top of his head, stopping at the nape of his neck.

He lowers his lashes before shifting his blue gaze to meet mine. "Gratitude is a stoic expla-nation, falling incredibly short of how I feel to be here now, with you. My life was obliterated and I felt every second of it. It changed me. I welcomed the onslaught. That, I deserved that." Before I can tell him he did not, he lifts his hand to silence me. "It's the presumptuous-ass method of moving through life. Blame and rage controlled me. But that's not what I see in you. That conversation we had last night—Avery, you still have hope. It still beats in your chest and sparkles in your eyes. That unyielding desire to share life, that you think it's a blessing. You changed me."

"I put you through hell." My gaze drops to my hands as I thread my fingers together. The memories of all the ways I've hurt him rush at me in an unyielding flash. The lump in my throat tightens.

His hand comes near, and he puts a finger under my chin, pulling me back toward him. "You freed me from hell. And I'll do the same for you. I promise. Nothing you can say or do will scare me off. I'm not going anywhere." He kisses my forehead and pulls me into his chest, hugging me.

The reassurance I needed to hear. The man has this innate quality of knowing what I need to hear and when to say it. It's a weakness that he can read me so easily, but shutting him out is the last thing I want to do.

Bashful, I smile up at him. That's what you get when the old me and the new me collide—blushes. I try to hide them, but I can't. And it's happening more and more lately. "What if I told you something? Something I wanted to do to you."

This new line of questioning piques his interest. "Oh? And what would that be Miss Smith?"

Pressing my lips together, I decide to tell him. It's a way to see if I want to go there with him again. If I want to be the one that brings this back into our bed. I lean into his ear and slip my tongue over my lips, saying the one thing that's been going through my mind since he sat down. My cheeks burn as I confess, and the pit of my stomach swirls at the words.

Sean has a serene smile on his face and knows to keep his gaze forward while I speak. He soaks in my confession and after a moment of silence, he glances at me. "That's what you want? Teeth?"

My entire face burns as I hide in the crook of his neck. As if someone else could hear. "Yes. And you. Tied to the chair. And me. Between your legs doing whatever I want."

His lips twitch and before I can finish what I'm saying, I can see that he likes the idea. His boxer briefs hug every inch of him, presenting me with a rather large compliment. "That sounds, well, you can see how it sounds." He shifts on the couch, aroused.

"Really?"

"Avery," he glances at me with an incredulous smile on his lips. It tugs at the corners every so slightly, not in mocking laughter, but amazement. "You could literally do anything to me and I'd let you. I'd love to see where this takes you. I'd love to be the one you rage on, the one who frees you from it. And it's not because turnabout is fair play. It's because I want to walk that path with you, if you'll let me. I want to see where you go, what you choose because I love you. Picket fences, piggy kites, dollar menus, and this provocative possession you want to exert over me. I want you. All of you." His hand rests on my cheek in a gesture of reassurance.

I nod and shift my gaze to the side, no longer trying to repress a shy smile. "You aren't worried I'll break? That this path ends in destruction?"

"Trust yourself, Avery. I do. With every ounce of my being. You're stronger than you realize, more ferocious than tame, and that's exactly what you need to be right now. Do you really not see how that fits with being a young mother?"

I blink at him, astounded. My brows knit together as I think about it. "No, I didn't see that at all." I was too busy hiding my feelings about this from him. Too upset thinking I've turned into a deviant. That I'm not the soft, pliant woman I once was. Okay, now I'm lying to myself. I've never been completely bendable. I've always held back part of me, and this throws it all out there. No hiding anything, because that kind of sex is dripping with emotions for me.

"Tell me what you want, Avery."

The corners of my lips tip up in a playful smirk. "You. Now."

CHAPTER 9

I rest my hand on my twins just in time to feel a tiny foot slam into my lower rib. I wince and close my eyes. My due date came and went. I'd jump on a trampoline if I thought I could roll out of this bed.

Sean's jaw is covered in dark stubble, his hair longer these days than when we first met. It falls over his forehead, past his eyebrows, and just reaches his dark lashes. His lips pull into a smile. "It's been over forty weeks of compliments. My repertoire is thin these days."

I can't help it. I want to pout. I try to fold my arms over my chest, but that's enormous too, so I basically hit myself in the face with my forearms. Grumbling, I mutter obscenities as Sean inches closer, strokes a hand across my face. "You're almost there, Avery."

Glancing up at him, our eyes meet. I know this is the beginning of a new life for us. Everything starts over here. It's a chance to heal old wounds and begin fresh. I want that more than anything. The thought of childbirth no longer frightens me. I want to hold these little girls in my arms and smile at them.

"Do you think they'll look like me or you?" I ask as I slip my arms around him and pull him close.

Sean barks a laugh, "They better look like you. A woman with this face would be awful." He teases me, says other things to make me smile, and then stands. We have names selected, perfect baby girl names.

Sean pads across the room and pulls open the curtains, knowing how much I love the sunlight, and how miserable it's been to be trapped in this bed for the past few weeks. Bedrest sucks. Sean stands with his back to me, looking through the handblown glass. The sunlight flashes on his naked body in curved pieces of light. The strength of his back, all the way down to that toned butt, and muscular legs that look so appealing.

My mind wanders to what my body looked like before and how it's a train wreck now. Before I know what happened, I'm blubbering about how beautiful he is and how fat I am—I sound like a hormonal mess.

Sean is there, sitting with me again, stroking my brow, kissing my cheek, and telling me things I didn't realize. "Do you know how hard it's been to keep my hands off of you?"

"You're just saying that."

He smiles sheepishly. "I swear, I'm not. The idea of fucking my pregnant wife is intoxicating. When the doc said hands off, I thought I'd die. Avery, these past few months have been more difficult for me than you could imagine. I know how horrible you feel, but it's like your beauty has been amplified. Your sexiness is off the charts. I mean look at these." He slides the pad of his finger down the side of my chest, following the generous sweep of my breast. His gaze is hot, lingering like he wants to dip his head and devour me.

"I miss you." The confession is off my lips before I have time to think about it. We never talked about this part because we couldn't do it.

"God, I want you." He buries his face in my breasts and then presses his body against mine.

"I heard sex can induce labor?" It sounds like a question.

Sean lifts his head and locks his eyes on mine. "I know. Do you really want to?"

"Do you really find this," I gesture to my massive self, "appealing?"

A deep growl rumbles through his chest in an answer. Then his lips are on me, moving, relearning the shape of my body, and the swell of my belly. I'm lost in his kisses, not worrying for once. This is different. I didn't know how I'd feel about it and didn't think we'd have a chance. It's past the due date.

Kissing. Touching. And then sharp stabbing pain. I press my hand to my belly, jerk upright, and gasp. Sean backs away, watching me. "Are you all right?"

I nod slowly as the pain fades. "Yeah. Fake contraction."

"How long has that been going on?"

"A couple of weeks."

He leans in cautiously. Kisses my neck once, and asks, "Do you want me to stop?"

I shake my head. "I miss you, and the contractions are fake—Braxton-Hicks thingies." Sean grins as if he knows something I do not. Cocking my head to the side, I try to convince him further, "Seriously. They're so far apart that it doesn't matter—" my word catches as another sharp pain hits which causes me to catch my breath. I lean forward, hand on belly, and press my eyes shut to endure the stab of pain.

When I open my eyes, Sean sits up beside me, grinning ear to ear. "I think it's baby time, Miss Smith."

Do NOT miss Sean, Avery, & BABIES?
THE ARRANGEMENT 26 is coming!
Text HMWARD (one word) to 24587
to receive a text reminder on release day.

Thank you to all the amazing readers who helped shape this series into a worldwide phenomenon.

Recently, a **NEW prologue** was added to THE ARRANGEMENT 1. You can download it for FREE by clicking here.

Thank you for reading!

ALL THE BROKEN PIECES

BY H.M. WARD

Turn the page to read a free sample of the new series by *New York Times* bestselling author H.M. Ward. All The Broken Pieces is a suspenseful, dark, and sexy Ferro tale.

ALL THE BROKEN PIECES: THE
FERRO FAMILY

*L*ONG ISLAND, NEW YORK
Hovering over my gradebook, I'm lost in thought and dreading the next part of my day. It's early afternoon and somehow communicating with parents via social media has become normal—expected. The problem? Facebook is so excited to see me when I login that it blasts me with pictures from my past, photographs of Zach's beautiful smiling face. Or memories of me and Zara. My arm around my best-friends shoulder.

A shiver runs over my skin. Pressing my hand to my forearm, I smooth the pebbled skin. Erasing the ghosts. There's a point where memories become so real, so inexplicably tangible, that it's as if those days never happened. My life would have been different if Zara and Zach lived. But they didn't. This is my life now.

My fingers hover over the keys of the laptop. Facebook is a graveyard where the dead still live. The family didn't want to delete their pages after their passing, which is understandable. Albeit painful for me. I'd never visit this site again if I had my way. But that's not the way the world works. So, Facebook pops Zach up in my feed as if nothing happened. As if he's still alive and breathing next to his twin sister, Zara. The weight in the center of my chest increases tenfold. It's to the point I should cave-in.

Maybe if only one of them died, then I could handle things better. But losing both? Within twelve months? It's too much. My soul tore in half. I walk amongst the living but I'm dead inside. Zara went first. She died about a year before Zach. His twin. I met him because of her. She was my college roommate. He was her devastatingly beautiful brother.

Now they're both ashes.

My throat is dry. I can't swallow. The students sit on stools at slanted desks with their pencils and drawing pads. They murmur amongst themselves as I stare at the screen, too afraid to press ENTER. No one is watching me. The kids don't notice, not really. I know I need to do it before the bell rings. Then my peers will be in the halls, and someone always walks in when I'm fracturing. My pointer hovers over the ENTER key. The URL is typed into the bar, cursor blinking. Waiting.

No matter how many times I experience it and no matter how much I prepare, I can't stomach it. If anything has a ghost in the program, it's social media. Zach's account glitches sometimes and there is movement on his wall. A blue dot showing a new message next to Zach's face lights up in my inbox. Unread.

Both were glitches. Cruel, heart-wrenching technological fails. I can't take much more. I've built a steel cage around my heart and let my soul wither and die—but in the split second of hope that fills my body, my grief falls away. Brimming with rekindled love, I click the private message only to realize it is old. The note was written before he died. Something happens after that and it's not pretty.

Goddamn school district. I stiffen in my

seat as a student nears my desk at the front of the classroom. Large windows frame the young woman. She's my little prodigy, Aleigha Thamas. Her dark eyes meet mine as rosy lips pull into a shy smile. She's clutching her drawing pad to her chest. I told the class to draw clouds today. Partly because grades are due, partly because I need their backs turned in case I get emotionally impaled on a Facebook picture when I send their parents invitations to the spring program.

"Ms. Abby?" In a southern school there would be no issue with the students calling me this. It shows respect, but in the north it's super weird. I can't remember when I changed it, when I asked the first student to stop calling me Ms. Sabba and use my first name instead.

The months have blurred into years, but a bleeding heart doesn't recognize time. The only way I know it's passing is when report cards are due or summer is looming, like now. I dread those months of nothing to do, of being assaulted by memories that I can't control.

I glance up at the student, glad to look away from the laptop for a moment. I tuck a strand of dark hair behind my ear. It wasn't out of place. "Yes, what can I help you with?"

"I was wondering what you thought of this

—" Her gaze cuts to the side mid-sentence and I know she's nervous about whatever she drew.

I reach out for her notepad and when I look down at the creamy paper, I'm surprised. There's a page of clouds, but instead of pencil lines and strokes each ball of mist is made of a string of zeros and ones. It looks like computer coding, all strings of numbers that may mean something to techies, but not me. I take a wild guess, "Is this binary?"

She ducks her head, hiding her face behind a wall of hair. "Not really. Well, maybe a little. I was thinking how cool it would be if the clouds could be drawn as molecules, but I didn't have my science textbook with me, so I switched to coding. Is it dumb?" Her face scrunches as uncertainty floods her features.

The one thing the girl lacks is confidence. No one ever told her that she was any good, so she's the last person to see it when she succeeds.

"This is amazing." I grasp her notepad between my hands and stare at it. The composition and flow are amazing. The fact that she did it with numbers and shading is even more entrancing. I tip the sketchpad sideways and tilt my head, admiring her work. "I don't know that much about coding. Do you?" I glance up at her.

She shakes her head. "Not really. I saw my brother messing around with something yesterday and I thought it might look cool. Robot clouds." She offers me an uncertain lopsided grin.

I hand her back her sketchpad. "You are amazing at conceptual execution. You remained true to the subject matter while infusing it with something different." Smiling softly, I add, "It feels like geo warning."

Her face lights up. "It does?"

"Yes, is that what you were hoping to achieve?" She nods fervently. "Well, go finish it up before the bell rings. You're onto something." She represses a grin as she crosses the room to peer out the window once more.

When she's settled on her stool once more with her back toward me and eyes fixed on the clouds, I return to gathering my guts to sign into Facebook. It's now or never. All eyes are on the sky and nowhere near me.

Slipping my finger across the touch pad on my laptop, I click open a browser and login.

The mental chanting has started, cycling endlessly:

Ignore the pictures.

Don't look.

I go straight to the school's page, click events, and start typing, entering the information for the High School Spring Art Program. After I've entered the details and invited the parents, I close the event window.

My feed is filled with ancient heartaches—Zara's smiling face looks out at me with her sun-kissed arm draped over my shoulder. The photograph was taken nearly four years ago. She was closer than any friend could be and was a sister in every way, even before Zach and I got married. She should have been at our wedding. She should have been laughing, walking up and down these hallways with me. But it never happened.

I scroll down. I can't help it. I've been sucked into the black hole. Pictures I've seen before fill the frame and I drink them in greedily. The emotion of past moments, the echoes of laughter long silenced, fills my mind.

My shrink, Dr. Roku would tell me this is unhealthy. That I should stop. No one ever walked forward while constantly looking back. It's the reason I can't seem to move on with my life. The reason for the unending nightmares. Maybe so.

I sigh deeply and rest my finger on the down button, watching the promises of a former lifetime of happiness scroll by in a blur. When I blink, the page refreshes and a new image is at the top. I'm staring at the screen, thinking I'm seeing a picture from a long time ago.

Zach stands there, beautifully ripped chest with chiseled abs wearing nothing but faded boardshorts. He grins at the camera in the sandy surf in Grand Cayman. A honeymoon picture. Every inch of his shirtless body is sun-kissed. A bronzed god. Dark hair ruffled from the wind as he ties a boat to the dock. Dread fades.

Curiosity rises in my chest. I don't recall this shot. Where were we? I must have taken it, but I don't remember. We were supposed to go out on a boat, but that's not the vessel. And that's not that dock we reported to for the dive. The long wooden wharf in this picture is weather worn and old. Splintering in patches and sun-bleached. The place where we were supposed to leave to go diving had silver-colored aluminum planks, almost blinding in the sun.

I click on the image and make it larger. Zach is bent forward, his face obscured slightly by the tips of his dark hair as he bends over to tie the boat to the dock.

That's when I see it.

The shiny spot on his arm.

I double click, enlarging the image as big as it can go, thinking it's sunscreen—assuming I took this picture but can't remember. As my eyes sweep the light patch of skin, I instinctively know what it's from, what I'm seeing.

"No," the word comes out in a puff of air.

Hands shaking, I jerk away from the laptop, toppling it to the floor. Eyes wide, my skin flushes as I stagger backwards, reaching for the wall, the counter, anything. Gaping, my mouth opens wide trying to suck in air. I can't breathe.

It's not possible.

* * *

PRE-ORDER *ALL THE BROKEN PIECES* NOW

COMPLETED SERIES BY
H.M. WARD

ROMANCE

~SECRETS & LIES~

~STRIPPED~

~THE PROPOSITION~

~DAMAGED~

~LIFE BEFORE DAMAGED~

~SECRETS~

~SECRET LIFE OF TRYSTAN SCOTT~

~SCANDALOUS~

TEEN PARANORMAL

~DEMON KISSED~

Please turn the page for a suggested reading order.

SUGGESTED FERRO READING
ORDER

THE ARRANGEMENT 1

THE ARRANGEMENT 2

THE ARRANGEMENT 3

THE ARRANGEMENT 4

THE ARRANGEMENT 5

THE ARRANGEMENT 6

DAMAGED 1

DAMAGED 2

SECRET LIFE OF TRYSTAN SCOTT 1

SECRET LIFE OF TRYSTAN SCOTT 2

SECRET LIFE OF TRYSTAN SCOTT 3

SECRET LIFE OF TRYSTAN SCOTT 4

SECRET LIFE OF TRYSTAN SCOTT 5

THE ARRANGEMENT 7

THE ARRANGEMENT 8

THE ARRANGEMENT 9

THE ARRANGEMENT 10

THE ARRANGEMENT 11

SCANDALOUS 1

SCANDALOUS 2

CAN'T WAIT FOR H.M. WARD'S NEXT STEAMY BOOK?

Let her know by leaving stars and telling her what you liked about this book in a review!

EXCITING MOVIE NEWS

HOW YOU CAN SEE SEAN FERRO IN THE FLESH!

*W*e've come a long way, Ferro fans! Movies are made by teams of folks who all work together to create the best film possible. It's not a one-man show.

Our next step is to obtain the best production company possible. We need a stellar team to bring the Ferro men to life. This is not an easy task. As you know, and love, the Ferro family has a dark side. You've spoken loudly to retain that element. Finding a perfect match is difficult. Especially since Ferro isn't mainstream romance.

There is a company that appears to be a proper fit—*Netflix*. They have several dark programs that resonate at the same frequency as the Ferro family.

Let *Netflix* know you want Sean, Peter, and the Ferro clan to come to life.

DIRECTIONS:

There are 3 slots on the form. **Use all 3 for the Ferro guys. This will give us the best shot at grabbing their attention**.

These are the forerunners for you to suggest. I'm suggesting these titles for a *specific* reason. They cover all our bases. It's possible there is a slot for Nick Ferro right now and something will open up for Sean later. We don't know exactly what they're looking for at this time.

The point is to give them the range of the Ferro books.

GO HERE TO TELL THEM YOU WANT TO SEE THE FERRO MEN: https://help.netflix.com/en/titlerequest

Enter the titles as shown below (**include author name** or they could choose another book with the same title):

Title Suggestion 1: **THE ARRANGEMENT** by H.M. Ward
Title Suggestion 2: **DAMAGED** by II.M. Ward
Title Suggestion 3: **THE WEDDING CONTRACT** by H.M. Ward

Then click SUBMIT SUGGESTIONS. It's a really simple thing you can do that will help the Ferro family come to life.

This is YOUR series.

Go make your suggestions NOW.

VOTE FOR THE NEXT FERRO BOOK

 OTE NOW! Want another book in THE ARRANGEMENT series?

VOTE NOW:

USA: Text **FERRO** to **24587**

INTERNATIONAL: Go post on my Facebook page at www.Facebook.com/AuthorHMWard.

This is a fan-driven series. Your vote matters, so go cast your vote now!

ABOUT H.M. WARD

H.M. Ward continues to reign as a *New York Times* bestselling author who sold 13+ million copies of her books worldwide, placing her among the literary titans.

Ward has been featured in articles in the NEW YORK TIMES, FORBES, and USA TODAY to name a few.

This native New Yorker resides in Texas with her family, where she enjoys painting and working on her next book.

You can interact with this bestselling author at:
www.hmward.com